To Cerri, on your Birthday 1993.
With Love, from, Hannah.

To John Lynch

Kingfisher Books, Grisewood & Dempsey Ltd,
Elsley House, 24–30 Great Titchfield Street,
London W1P 7AD

First published in 1991 by Kingfisher Books

BRITISH LIBRARY CATALOGUING IN PUBLICATION DATA
Jordan, Martin, *1944–*
Ronnie the red-eyed tree frog.
I. Title   II. Jordan, Tanis
823.914 |J|
ISBN 0 86272 842 8

Designed by Terry Woodley
Phototypeset by Waveney Typesetters, Norwich
Colour separations by Newsele Litho, Milan, London
Printed in Hong Kong

RONNIE
The Red-Eyed Tree Frog

Martin and Tanis
Jordan

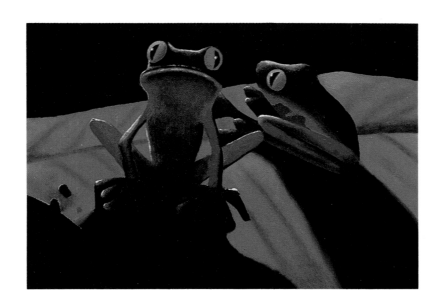

Kingfisher Books

Deep in the Forest of Central America, in the middle of a river, is a happy, peaceful place called Treefrog Island. In the big Purpleheart Tree live two tiny Red-Eyed Tree Frogs. Every morning a pair of Keel-Billed Toucans that lived on the mainland stopped by.

"You know, you two look so alike we can never tell which is which," they said together.

"But it's obvious," said the frogs. "I'm Ronnie," said Ronnie, and "I'm Mabel," said Mabel.

It was on the first day of March that the trouble began. Ronnie and Mabel woke up to a world full of smoke. It made Ronnie sneeze and Mabel's eyes sting until they watered.

"What's going on?" said Ronnie to the Toucans, who arrived in a panic.

"It's the people! They are burning down the forest!" they cried. "We were asleep, we only just flew away in time!"

Ronnie and Mabel were frightened by the fire.

"Why are they burning the

forest?" cried Ronnie. "It's hot enough living here without great roaring fires all over the place."

"I know who can tell us!" exclaimed Mabel. "The Atlantic Golden Plover always calls in on her way back to Canada. She knows a thing or two about the world, we'll ask her."

A week later, when the Plover arrived, the damage was done.

"Eeek! The people are making a cattle ranch," she clucked. "Oh dear, oh dear, this is very bad news. Everywhere I fly I see more and more big bare patches of land that used to be forests. I'm very worried about it all, very worried indeed. I'm sorry to have to tell you," Plover said, "that Treefrog Island could be next for the chop!"

Ronnie and Mabel were thunderstruck.

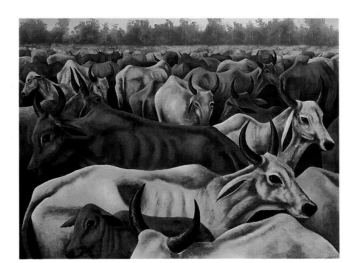

"But they can't burn the Purpleheart Tree, it's our home!" they gasped.

"The problem is," continued Plover, "that the cattle never stop eating and they're munching nearer all the time.

They will eat us out of bushes and trees."

"Well," said Ronnie firmly, "they are not going to munch up Treefrog Island. Somehow we must save it."

"But what are the cattle for?" chorused the Toucans, who'd been listening.

"To eat, to eat, the people eat them," explained Plover.

The Frogs gulped and the Toucans blinked twice with astonishment.

"I have an idea," said the Plover. "Deep in the Amazon forests lives the fount of all wisdom, the Oracle Toad. You must make an expedition to find him, Ronnie. He will tell you what to do."

"But I'm only two inches big!" exclaimed Ronnie, looking up in surprise.

"You are big in courage," said the Plover, "and that's what matters."

Leaving Mabel in charge of the island, Ronnie found a strong leaf, placed it on the shimmering river and climbed on. His journey had begun.

Three days later a boat full of noisy people chugged by. Although Ronnie clung to his leaf with all his toes he was swished into the churning river.

"Pooh!" said Ronnie, hauling himself back onto his leaf. The water was oily and smelly and covered with bubbles of

brown scum. On the riverbank, instead of trees there were factories with tall chimneys belching smoke into a grey sky. So this was where the people lived. He didn't feel safe to sleep until he was way beyond the town.

Ronnie woke up on a beach. Close by sat a Green Turtle and a Fiddler Crab.

"Excuse me," Ronnie said to the Crab, "Why have you one big claw and one little claw?"

"Good question. When seagulls attack me, I threaten them with the big claw. If that doesn't scare them, I hide in my hole in the ground and block the entrance with it."

Ronnie turned to the Turtle. "Is this the Amazon River, please?"

"My dear child," said Turtle, "this isn't a river, this is the Pacific Ocean, the biggest ocean in the world." She drew a map in the sand with her flipper. "You are here and you've still got about one thousand miles to go."

"A thousand miles!" Ronnie was horrified.

"Come along," said Turtle kindly, "I can help you some of the

way. You can sit on my head and I will swim you to Peru."

The sea journey was long and harsh. Despite the spray from the waves, it was horribly hot. At night the wind blew and it was cruelly cold. But at last the good Turtle delivered him safely to the coast of Peru. A tear slid from her eye.

"Why are you crying?" said Ronnie.

"These are special tears to wash out the extra salt I soak up from the sea," answered Turtle, smiling. "Good luck, Ronnie."

Ronnie set off up the beach. Among the driftwood was a peculiar-looking object, with a hole at one end. Ronnie crept inside. It was smooth and clean and he could see out in all directions. At that moment, the shadow of a huge bird with the longest, spindliest legs he had ever seen, fell across the sand. It was a Jabiru Stork.

"You are a very silly frog!" announced the Jabiru.

Ronnie gazed up at this giant, fierce-looking bird with its glittering eyes. It could gobble up Ronnie and the object without a hiccup.

"Do you not realize that you are inside a bottle made of glass? Glass shatters into sharp dangerous splinters. Creatures get cut and injured, even killed, by glass that people throw all over the place. Come out at once."

"You're not going to eat me, are you?" Ronnie asked with a tremor in his voice.

"Well I was," said the Jabiru, "but you look poisonous to me."

"I am, I am," said Ronnie, who isn't, "I'm so poisonous that if you eat me you'll be horribly, miserably sick."

"I think that's rather an exaggeration," said the Jabiru, "but I don't want to risk indigestion. I had seven frogs and five fish for breakfast. However, if you're still here at teatime –"

"Oh I won't be, I must find the abode of the Oracle Toad. Can you direct me to the Amazon River, please?" asked Ronnie, climbing out of the bottle.

"The Amazon! Just how do you propose to get there? Where are your wings?" the Jabiru scoffed.

"I've got to get there," Ronnie declared. "Everyone at Treefrog Island is depending on me!"

"Are they indeed? Well, little frog, you may be tiny but you have the courage of a jaguar, king of the forests. And you will need it, for you must cross a great range of mountains called the Andes. It will be a long, cold climb and I wish you a safe journey."

Ronnie climbed through the snowy mountains until he thought his feet would drop off with the cold. He knew that if he fell asleep in the snow he would freeze to death. In the distance he saw a swirl of smoke coming from the chimney of a stone hut. He dragged his tired body toward it and with a superfrog effort he crawled inside.

As his eyes became accustomed to the gloom, he saw three furry shapes huddled together. "Help!" he cried. "Please help. I'm as cold as a block of ice."

The creatures leapt up and began racing around, squeaking. "Wh-what on earth are you?" asked one.

"I'm a frightened, frosty forest frog with frozen feet," said Ronnie.

The big white Guinea Pig gently pushed Ronnie across the floor towards the others. Snuggled against them, he defrosted and fell asleep.

Next morning, they told Ronnie how to get to the

Amazon River. "First you go down through the snow and the rocks until you come to where grass grows. Further down you'll see clouds floating in the tree-tops. This is the Cloud Forest. It's wet and tangly with vines and creepers and the ground is covered with squishy, squelchy moss. Further down the mountain you'll find many kinds of gigantic trees. Even the Oracle Toad cannot count how many different kinds there are in the Amazon forests."

Ronnie leapt nervously from tree to tree. "The Guinea Pigs were right," he thought, "there could be anything hiding in this Cloud Forest and I wouldn't see it until it was right in front of me."

"HELLOOOO!" roared a deep voice. A massive animal reared up out of the undergrowth. If it hadn't been for the sticky pads on his toes Ronnie would have fallen flat on his front with fright.

"I'm most dreadfully sorry," apologized the animal, "but you're such a tidgy thing I didn't see you until you were right in front of me. I'm a Spectacled Bear, who are you?"

"I'm a Red-Eyed Tree Frog and I'm looking for the Oracle Toad," said Ronnie.

"I can't help you there," said the Bear, "I rarely leave the Cloud Forest. You could ask the Owls – they're supposed to be very wise."

The Spectacled Bear climbed up to his nest at the top of a tree and Ronnie continued his journey down the mountainside. That night several Owls and a Night Monkey came to look at him.

"The Spectacled Bear said that you are the wisest of creatures," said Ronnie. The Owls watched silently. "Well," he continued, "as you are so wise, perhaps you can tell me where to find the Oracle Toad?"

"Hooo," said the Big Horned Owl.

"The Oracle Toad," said Ronnie.

"Hooo, hooo," said the Owl.

"The Oracle Toad, the Oracle Toad," said Ronnie, louder.

"Hooo, hooo, hooooo," said another Owl, leaning forward.

"What's the matter with them?" asked Ronnie, turning to the Night Monkey in dismay. "Are they deaf?"

"Deaf! Definitely not," said the Night Monkey, "they just like to tease. They have extra-special hearing and extra-special eyesight. Like me," she added proudly. "I am a Douracouli and Douracoulis are the only monkeys who are out and about at night. That's why I have such big eyes and –"

"Follow the stream to find the Toad," interrupted the Horned Owl, "you must follow the stream until it becomes a wide river, but not too far, for all rivers lead to the sea."

Ronnie continued his journey, leaping from tree to tree. Suddenly he was nose to beak with a Vulture, ferociously waggling the wattle on its head.

"Oh boy, bags I get to eat him," said the huge Harpy Eagle, flexing his enormous talons.

The Scarlet Macaw scratched under her wing with her sharp, hooked beak. "I couldn't bear to eat him. I don't understand how you eagles can eat live frogs. Personally, I wouldn't touch anything but fruit and nuts."

"He looks a tasty morsel. I just love foreign food. Can I eat him now?" The Harpy Eagle lunged at Ronnie.

"Not yet!" screamed the Hyacinth Macaw. "We don't know where he's been." The Tufted Coquette fluttered around Ronnie, jabbing at him with her thin pointed beak. "Or where he's going."

"OK shrimp, what have you got to say for yourself before Harpy here has you for breakfast?" asked the Vulture.

Ronnie took a deep breath. "I am seeking the abode of the Oracle Toad to save Treefrog Island."

"Very commendable," said the Harpy Eagle. "*Now* can I eat him?"

"No, no," said the Vulture, "first tell us how you plan to find the Oracle Toad?"

"I'm to follow the stream till it's a big river," said Ronnie.

Vulture winked at Harpy Eagle. "He's all yours!"

The Harpy Eagle clutched Ronnie in his sharp talons. He flapped his wings and took off, flying upside down between the trees. Ronnie felt quite sick. He was going to end up as breakfast for this nasty bird. "OK pipsqueak, this is the Amazon River. The Oracle Toad is somewhere around here," said the Eagle, gently setting Ronnie down.

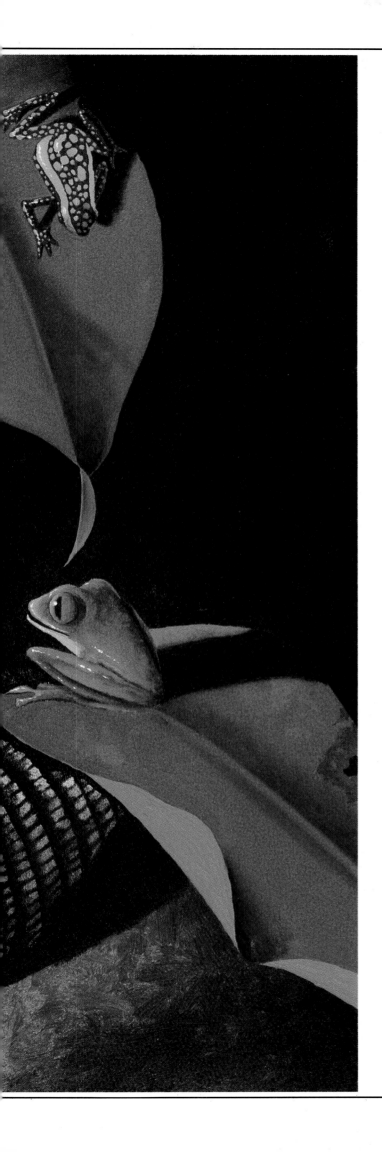

"Then you're not going to eat me?" cried Ronnie with relief.

"Oh, come on," said the Harpy Eagle indignantly, "I am a giant among birds of prey. I fly upside down so I can snatch magnificent monkeys and sedentary sloths from the trees. I'd have to be starving to resort to a frog as small as you!"

Ronnie sat by the wide river. At daybreak a scaly creature came shuffling along.

"Good morning," said Ronnie.

"What and who, may I ask, are you?" the Armadillo demanded.

"I'm a Red-Eyed Tree Frog," announced Ronnie proudly, "the most colourful frog in the world. I'm an explorer, too."

"Huh!" snorted the Armadillo, "the most colourful frog in the world, eh? And an explorer too! Well, well, you haven't explored very far, have you? Just look over there!"

Ronnie looked, and gulped. The Amazon frogs had come to see him. As colourful as jelly babies, they positively shone at Ronnie and chirruped and croaked, warbled and whistled, gargled and glugged.

All Ronnie could do was give his

single faint beep. He crept away, feeling drab.

"I don't care," thought Ronnie as he hopped along, "Mabel thinks I'm lovely." He was so busy thinking about Mabel that he didn't see the big hairy hand that reached out and grabbed him. The gnome-like creature looked like a monkey, but its head was bald and as red as a tomato. Ronnie thought it was the funniest, ugliest, most peculiar thing he had ever seen.

"I'm a Red-faced Uakari," said the Monkey, "and I suppose you think I'm the funniest, ugliest, most peculiar thing you've ever seen."

"No! No, I don't," said Ronnie guiltily, "I think you are a most spendid U . . . Uak . . ."

"Wackery, you say it like wackery," said the Uakari. "Do you know that I was once described in a book as having a 'grotesquely dishevelled look, with an entirely hairless head, and a scarlet face that gets redder if I get excited'? I thought that was very rude," said the Uakari, getting redder and redder, "after all, none of us can help how or what we were born. It's unkind to laugh at other creatures, isn't it?"

Suddenly, from the branch above came a roar so loud that Ronnie leapt straight out of the Uakari's hand. "Take no notice of him," whispered the Uakari. "Just because he's got a louder voice than anyone else he thinks he's important."

"I AM IMPORTANT," roared the Howler Monkey. "AND YOU'D BETTER TAKE NOTICE OF ME! IT'S MY JOB TO WAKE YOU ALL UP IN THE MORNINGS. WITHOUT ME YOU WOULD ALL SLEEP UNTIL NINE O'CLOCK!"

Ronnie's ears were still ringing when he climbed a
Cecropia Tree for a better view of the river. At the top, a
Sloth hung motionless from a vine, her baby snuggled
against her. Ronnie swung upside down to talk to her.

"Madam, do you know the abode of the Oracle Toad?"
Ronnie asked. With a great commotion and kerfuffle a Blue
and Yellow Macaw landed and swung upside down to talk
to Ronnie.

"It's no good asking her," squawked the Macaw,
plucking a feather from his tail, "she does everything so

slowly it would take her a week of Mondays to answer you. But I can tell you right now. The Oracle Toad is across the river."

Ronnie climbed down the tree and for the second time in his life he set sail on a leaf. Four fish with sharp, triangular teeth swam up. "What kind of fish are you?" asked Ronnie nervously.

"We are Piranhas. People say that we bite everyone who ventures into the river but it's simply not true. Some of us are actually vegetarians!"

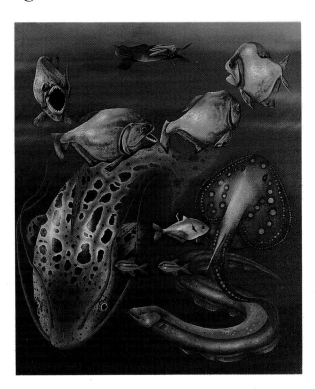

"*I* know how to handle people," said an Electric Eel. "They get a nasty shock if they come too near. *That* makes them stop and think."

"If a people treads on me, I wacks 'em wiv me tail. Makes 'em 'op around a bit, that does," said the Sting-ray.

"Well, I wouldn't hurt anybody even if I could," said Ronnie. "What I need is advice from the Oracle Toad." With a grunt and a splash a Giant Catfish nine feet long flicked its tail and sent Ronnie's leaf spinning across the water towards the bank. Three dazzling Tetra fish pushed Ronnie's leaf up a stream into a deep lagoon among the trees. Ronnie gazed into the water. There, looking right at him, was the reflection of a big, powerful cat. It was Jaguar, King of the forests. Behind him sat a Black Jaguar.

"Your Majesty, Your Highness," Ronnie bowed.

"It's all right, tiny one," said King Jaguar. "Remember I am no more important than you. All of us have a special part to play in the forest."

"I have come from Central America to find the abode of the Oracle Toad," said Ronnie. "Treefrog Island is threatened by the people and I need his advice."

"We are his guardians. He is expecting you. The Black Princess will take you to him at dawn tomorrow," said King Jaguar. "You may stay with us tonight. Don't worry, Prince Ocelot of Peru is on patrol."

That night they told Ronnie how poachers had tried to kill them to turn their skins into fur coats. "They set traps with vicious hooks concealed in lumps of meat," said the Black Princess, "they know it's our favourite food." Ronnie was shocked.

Just before dawn the Black Princess woke Ronnie. He clambered onto her back and she padded off through the inky blackness until she came to the river.

"Wait here until sunrise," she purred, "all will be revealed." She disappeared into the shadows.

Ronnie shivered with excitement. A thick, milky-white mist hung over the water. Swiftly the sun rose and the mist began to clear. And there at last, on a rock, sat the Oracle Toad.

"Come closer, Ronnie," he ordered with a booming croak. Ronnie hopped across to the rock. He had never seen such an awesome creature. The Oracle Toad's warty skin glowed amber in the dawn light.

"You have proved yourself to be a superfrog, Ronnie. You are brave and courageous and you do not deserve to lose your home."

"Will you help me?" begged Ronnie. The Oracle Toad's great golden eyes gazed over the river.

"I will see what I can do," he said. "Listen to me, Ronnie. There are good people who are fighting to save our forests so that *all* our homes will be safe. In the old days, when I was a tadpole, there were

animals galore. Now every day I hear of relatives and friends becoming extinct, disappearing forever. And all because of the people who treat our forests as if they are worthless, just places to raise cattle and make money. They don't seem to realize that once the forests are destroyed *nobody* knows what will happen to the world. The trouble with people is that there are too many of them, too many of them wanting too many things. However, they are here and what we must do is to try to educate them, to give them some of our natural wisdom. Then, they may learn to respect us. I will tell the people about your brave adventure, Ronnie," said the Oracle Toad. "Perhaps they will write a book about you."

"Will it be called Ronnie the Red-Eyed Tree Frog?" asked Ronnie.

"Yes."

Ronnie's red eyes widened. "Will it have pictures of me in it?"

"Yes."

"I just can't wait to tell Mabel!" said Ronnie.

The Oracle Toad waggled a toe and a bird swooped down from the top of a Brazilnut Tree. It was the Atlantic Golden Plover and she had come to carry Ronnie home.

As Plover flew him back to Treefrog Island, Ronnie's heart filled with happiness at the thought of seeing Mabel and all his friends again.

Ronnie had been away for a whole year and the Oracle Toad had kept his word. The good people had made Treefrog Island into a protected area. The cattle had gone and trees were starting to grow again.

Ronnie and Mabel sat on a leaf at sunset and the animals called up their thanks.

"You have made this a safer place for us to live," whistled the Tapir, nudging the young one who still had her baby spots and stripes. "Thank you Ronnie."

"Yeah, thanks Ron, thanks a lot," grunted one of the band of White Lipped Peccaries. "Not bad for a nipper."

Ronnie blushed with pride. "Mabel," he said, "whatever our future holds, I'm sure it will be full of adventure."

Treefrog Island was a happy and peaceful place once again.